I
I
always have fun
with you!
Love,
Riba

ARTCIDENT!

RIBA KALB

Illustrated by
GOLNAR SEPAHI

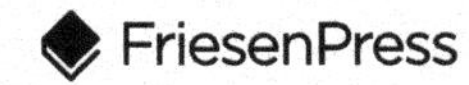

One Printers Way
Altona, MB R0G 0B0
Canada

www.friesenpress.com

First Edition — 2023

ISBN
978-1-03-916272-3 (Hardcover)
9781-03-916271-6 (Paperback)
978-1-03-916273-0 (eBook)

1. JUVENILE FICTION, SOCIAL ISSUES, EMOTIONS & FEELINGS

Distributed to the trade by The Ingram Book Company

To my husband. You are my rock.
To my kids and my mom. I love you all.
To all my students who have inspired me
to write this story.

Finally, it was summer. Taylor had been waiting and waiting for **ART** camp with Miss Brush.

"I'm so excited, Mom," said Taylor, on the first morning of camp.

But Taylor was a little worried, too—she hoped she would be good at the **ART** projects. She hated making mistakes. Whenever she did, her face turned red, and her eyes welled with tears.

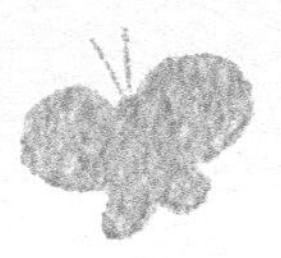

"Welcome, amazing **ARTISTS**," said Miss Brush.

"We're going to be together for a few days, doing all kinds of **surprising projects**." She smiled. "Now, close your eyes, use your **imagination**, and let's travel to the wonderful world of **ART**."

10

Taylor didn't close her eyes. She wasn't sure what Miss Brush wanted her to do, exactly. Her stomach was starting to churn.

"Now, open them and let's get started," said Miss Brush.

"Today, we are going to learn about **landscapes**," said Miss Brush.

"First, we make a nice, straight horizon line from one side to the other, to show where the earth meets the sky …

… **ARTCIDENT!**" yelled Miss Brush.

What is going on? thought Taylor, staring at Miss Brush's **picture**. ***That doesn't look right.*** Her eyes were wide with worry. Teachers can't make **mistakes**!

10

"I drew a curvy line instead of a straight line," said Miss Brush, laughing. "I love to make **mistakes**. I call them **ARTCIDENTS** and they're no problem. With a little bit of **imagination**, **accidents** in **ART** can help us have new and often better ideas. See—this curvy line can become a mountain in my **landscape**."

All the kids got started on their **landscapes**.

Suddenly, there was a soft scream. It came from Jack, who was two seats down from Taylor. He had tipped his water cup over.

"Miss Brush," said Jack, his voice full of disappointment, "I spilled water all over my **watercolor painting** of the night. Is it ruined?"

Taylor felt terrible for Jack and inched her own water cup further away from her **painting**. She didn't want that to happen to her.

Miss Brush smiled at Jack. "It's an ..."

"... **ARTCIDENT**?" said Jack.

"You're right, Jack,

ARTCIDENT! "confirmed Miss Brush.

Taylor made sure to be extra careful with her own **painting**.

"Jack?" asked Miss Brush, "How do you think you can solve this challenge?"

Mmmmm ... Jack was thinking. "Maybe I can use the paper towel to absorb the water?"

He tried it.

"Good idea!" said Miss Brush. "Look, you're turning night to dusk."

"Oh yeah," he said.

"Plus, dabbing with your paper towel is creating a **nice texture**," added Miss Brush.

"It looks better than before!" said Jack, admiring his **picture**.

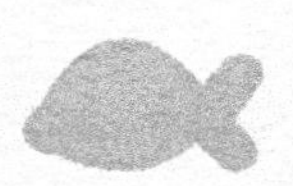

"Miss Brush?" said Liza, looking curious. "I'm drawing the ocean. But I got confused and I used a **MARKER** instead of an **OIL PASTEL**. Is that okay?"

Taylor quickly straightened her **supplies** on her desk.

She didn’t want that to happen to her.

Miss Brush smiled. "It's an . . ."

"**ARTCIDENT!**" said Liza, excitedly.

"No problem. I know what to do," said Liza.

"I'll use **OIL PASTELS** for the waves and **MARKERS** for the fish."

"Good idea!" said Miss Brush. "Don't forget, Liza, that you can also add some cut-outs of tissue paper for the ocean plants to make a **mixed media artwork**."

After a couple of days of working on the **landscape** project, they began working on **self-portraits.**

Miss Brush said, "Let's look at ourselves in the mirror. What is the **SHAPE** of your face, your eyes, and what is the **COLOR** of your hair? Investigate all your beautiful facial features. We are all different and that is what makes us special!

"And remember," she said, "it doesn't have to look exactly like you—you can transform yourself into something else."

“Miss Brush,” said Marcus, calmly, “I was about to make a thin line with my **BRUSH** to make the outline of my face with **INK** and my **BRUSH** dropped some big blobs on the paper.”

Taylor quickly double-checked her own **BRUSH** to make sure it had just the right amount of **PAINT** on it. She didn’t want that to happen to her.

Miss Brush smiled. “It’s an . . .”

“**ARTCIDENT!**” said Marcus.

He had a big smile on his face too.

“No problem, I know what to do,” said Marcus, confidently. “What if I transform the **INK** blobs into a monster’s eyes?!”

“Good idea!” said Miss Brush. “Remember, Marcus, that when the **INK** is dry, you can also use **OIL PASTELS** to add details to the eyes and make them special.”

"Miss Brush," said Natalie, eagerly, "I wanted to add the exact shape of my hands in my **self-portrait**. But when I was tracing them, I got distracted, and one of my fingers is way too big."

Taylor made sure to focus even more carefully on her work. She didn't want that to happen to her.

Artcident

Miss Brush smiled. “It’s an . . .”

“**ARTCIDENT!**” Natalie called out.

“No problem,” said Natalie. “If I complete my **drawing** and add more details, it will look like my hands are a butterfly. The long finger can become the body of the butterfly.”

“Good idea!” said Miss Brush. “If you like, the **COLORS** of your butterfly can be **complementary colors,** so they can **contrast** with one another and really **POP.**”

Taylor loved butterflies. She looked over at Natalie's **drawing** and had to admit that it was beautiful.

Oh no! While she was distracted by Natalie's **drawing,** something terrible happened to Taylor.

Her face turned red. Her eyes welled with tears.

"Miss Brush," said Taylor, very quietly.

"Yes, Taylor?" said Miss Brush, encouragingly.

"Instead of making a round shape for my face, I made a triangle. Can I start my **self-portrait** again on a new piece of paper?" asked Taylor, with a trembling voice.

Miss Brush smiled. “It’s an ...”

Taylor remembered the magic word Miss Brush and all Taylor’s friends were using.

“ART ... CIDENT?” she said, quietly.

“YES!”

“**ARTCIDENT!**” sang Taylor.

She wanted to make sure she said it right.

Taylor started to think. ***Maybe the triangle can become a hat on my face ... no ... maybe I can be inside of a house ... no ....*** But then she had an **idea**.

"No problem!" said Taylor, with a big sigh. "I will make my **self-portrait** as a robot. An **imaginary self-portrait** instead of a **realistic** one. I love robots."

"Good idea!" said Miss Brush, her eyes sparkling. "You can always use your **imagination** when you do **ART**."

After that moment, Taylor felt a sense of relief!

All through the rest of the **ART** camp, **ARTCIDENTS** kept coming.

Oli's **PAPER** had an old, oval stain on it. So, he made the oval into a bee and set his **self-portrait** in a **colorful** garden.

Bianca used so much water that her **PAPER** got a hole in it. So, she cut newspaper into **organic** and **geometric** **SHAPES** and added them as a **COLLAGE** for her **abstract** background, **painting** the **SHAPES** with **WATERCOLORS**.

It was close to the end of the very last day of **ART** camp when suddenly there was a loud noise.

SPLASH!

Everyone looked at Taylor. Everyone looked at the floor. All of Taylor's **RED, BLUE,** and **YELLOW** tempera **PAINT** had spilled on the floor.

Taylor, with a big, embarrassed smile, shouted,

"ARTCIDENT!"

"BIG ARTCIDENT!"

Everyone laughed.

No problem, thought Taylor. ***I will cover the spilled paint with a big piece of paper to make a print of the primary colors that are on the floor.***

She did just that. She grabbed the white paper and put it over the **PAINT**. When she lifted the paper, she couldn't believe how beautiful it looked. The **primary** and **secondary colors** had blended: **RED, BLUE, YELLOW, PURPLE, ORANGE,** and **GREEN.**

She lifted the **painting** up for everyone to see and confidently said, "The name of this **PAINTING** is **ARTCIDENT!**"

Miss Brush said, "Good job Taylor! **ARTCIDENTS** can be so much **fun**, right?"

TAYLOR just smiled.

The End

10

Artcident

About the Author

RIBA KALB has been teaching art to children aged two to nine for over thirty years, in both Canada and Mexico. She started to use the word "ARTCIDENT" in her classes around fifteen years ago. She found that it unfailingly helped children with their anxiety around making "ART accidents," and brought smiles to their faces. She believes that there is always a way to transform art errors in a fun way, and that there is no right or wrong in art—the important thing is for children to be able to enjoy art and express themselves. "ARTCIDENT" has become a popular word with other teachers in her school and even with some parents.

Riba works at Arts Umbrella, an Art & Design, Dance, and Theatre School for children in Vancouver, and at Vancouver Talmud Torah School. She lives in Vancouver, Canada, with her husband. She has three adult children.

CPSIA information can be obtained
at www.ICGtesting.com
Printed in the USA
LVHW051612170223
739754LV00005B/10